Anchor Of Destiny

Bright Mills

Ukiyoto Publishing

All global publishing rights are held by

Ukiyoto Publishing

Published in 2023

Content Copyright © Bright Mills

ISBN 9789360162184

All rights reserved.
No part of this publication may be reproduced, transmitted, or stored in a retrieval system, in any form by any means, electronic, mechanical, photocopying, recording or otherwise, without the prior permission of the publisher.

The moral rights of the author have been asserted.

This is a work of fiction. Names, characters, businesses, places, events, locales, and incidents are either the products of the author's imagination or used in a fictitious manner. Any resemblance to actual persons, living or dead, or actual events is purely coincidental.

This book is sold subject to the condition that it shall not by way of trade or otherwise, be lent, resold, hired out or otherwise circulated, without the publisher's prior consent, in any form of binding or cover other than that in which it is published.

www.ukiyoto.com

About the Book

The best seller book entitled, Anchor of Destiny, is another intriguing short fiction stories made up of three books; The Great Betrayal, Dark Heart, and The Accountant. The great betrayal is about pastor Ishan and his wife Navi, who pastor a small community church in the heart of Chennai. Pastor was addicted to phone sex and wasted almost their household money on sex hot line. In order for his faithful wife not to expose him to the church and community, he murdered and buried her inside the bush. The book dark heart is about a woman who unknowingly fell in love with a murderer. She wanted to be the woman to change his life for the better but his criminal husband was have a terrifying secret. To kill her, and claimed her money and estate. The book, the accountant is about jewelry business owner who hired an accountant as his bookkeeper to join him perfect a Ponzi scheme, so that at the end, he will pour everything on her, make her disappear without trace and claimed she had made away with his fortunes, so that he can keep all the looted funds to himself.

Contents

The Great Betray	1
Chapter 1	2
Chapter 2	6
Chapter 3	10
Dark Heart	15
Chapter 1	16
Chapter 2	21
Chapter 3	24
The Accountant	28
Chapter 1	29
Chapter 2	34
Chapter 3	41
Chapter 4	48
About the Author	52

The Great Betray

Chapter 1

It was not long in the city of Chennai, the Indian capital of Tamil Nadu. Ishan Ahuja, and Navi Ahuja has made a full life in a rolling beautiful country side of Chennai, as a devoted Christian couple. There were really the idea of what you would expect from a Christian couple. Ishan is an ordained pastor in a local church in Chennai. He is a person that people really trust and trusted his judgement. Ishan's wife Navi is deeply involved in church work as well, and leads the community music program. She was very instrumental in the ministry of the church that is where she really focused her time. According to her niece Roja Patel, Navi has a remarkable voice. She has so much talent. She is very beautiful playing the piano.

Ishan and Navi has chosen a spiritual path in life and devote themselves to the ministry, and showing their faith. They said they wanted to help people as being their mission. They would go for missionary trips for the church, spreading the word of the gospel. However, in setting aside worldly pursuit, they also struggle financially, and Navi takes on cleaning job to help support them. Navi works in cleaning houses, making 2500 Rupees a week. She is doing everything she can as a nice daughter, and a nice Christian woman, dedicated to her church and family. She was a homemaker for her husband. As true-life partners, Navi believes their marriage is their spiritual journey on earth. They are not just married to each other, but are married to the Lord. And so there is three in this relationship. Moreover, that gives them a very different foundation. For Ishan and Navi, their whole life are dedicated to their faith. They are happily married and living in the city of Chennai. Chennai is the capital city of Tamil Nadu.

It is the political and cultural hub of Tamil Nadu and epitome of Dravidian movement in India. Chennai is referred as gateway to South India. It may not have a Red Fort or a Marine Drive or a

Victoria Memorial, but it is India's oldest modern city. There are several temples, churches, forts, mosques, palaces and natural attractions in Chennai. It is one of the four metropolitan cities of India and is the capital of Tamil Nadu. This state is famous for its beach, temples, fabrics, monuments, Carnatic music, classical dances, and food. It's an ancient city known for its culture, trade and architecture. Chennai have its mark during the colonial times of British and French. It's a small Asia where you can witness different kinds of people, cultures, and traditions. There is no wonder in calling Chennai as an exotic state as it preserves its deep-rooted traditions and age-old heritage.

Chennai is the cultural capital of South India. This 350 years old city has the vibe of young hearts. British had a stronghold on Madras during the independence era and did many good to the city. They were the prime reason for the drastic development of Chennai city, which was once just a forest land. The northern part of Chennai is primarily an industrial area, and the central part is the commercial heart of the city. Whereas South and west chennai are mostly residential areas. Kodambakkam is the cinema hub of Kollywood, filled with lots of film industries, studios and cinema sets. Irrespective of the metropolis heart, Chennai perfectly balances its old heritage and the modern vibe. It's a sight to behold the Chennai's skyline, which is brimming with skyscrapers. Once you were at Chennai you will quickly adapt to its hustle bustle and will tend to love its multi face.

Chennai Tourist Attractions. Kalakshetra: Kalakshetra Foundation, formerly simply Kalakshetra, is an arts and cultural academy dedicated to the preservation of traditional values in Indian art and crafts, especially in, Chennai, Tamilnadu, Kalakshetra – Chennai, Government Museum. The Madras Literary Society initiated the plan for this museum in 1846 AD and it was established on January 01, 1951. Cholamandal Artists Village – Chennai, Marina Beach, Chennai. Whitehaven beach's main attraction is the pure white silica sand, along a seven kilometre (four or five mile) stretch. The National Art Gallery, Chennai, is one of the oldest art galleries in India. This Gallery was built in 1906 in Indo-Sarsenic architecture and houses. Among cities in India with more than a million population, Chennai has the best quality of life, is highly resilient with best mobility options and is safe and secure. However, the city ranks poorly on economic abilities, places of recreation and the number of green structures.

There are regular church services, but from the moment they get out at the end of the day, they made himself or herself available for the work of the mission, counselling tanagers and young adults. Their door is always open. People love to hang out with them even at home. Ishan and Navi have a special commitment to their youth ministry. They believe they can make a big impact in young people who may be struggling with their faith. They even take students into their home, when church members ask for their mentorship. The community has given him the strong position of trust to lead and guide them. There is a huge expectation that he is leading them to the right direction. Ishan and Navi, are living a life of faith and helping others in need. For many people around them, they are the perfect Christian couples.

However, on June 12, 2002, Ishan world is suddenly breaking apart by a shocking event. Ehen Ishan returned home from a community play that night, he expects Navi to be home. Nevertheless, she is nowhere to be found. It is completely on like Navi to be late. As the hours tick by, Ishan becomes worried and calls the police. He made the first call by 12 midnight to the police, and the police asked him if he was sure that Navi has not left him. But Ishan said that he is very sure that she would never leave him. The next day, there is still no sign of Navi. Ishan was telling some members of his church that Navi his wife is missing. But nobody has any idea where his wife could be. The congregation is also worried.

 Navi is not someone who would just walk away from her life. They believe her love for Ishan is deep, and her commitment to doing God's work is unwavering. At one point in time, people were asking if Navi would run off. They believe that it would not happened without a doubt. Soon the people that knew her best started to have a terrible fear about what might have happened. The police started thinking, who could have kidnapped or killed Navi Ahuja. Who would have done such a thing to her? Four days after her disappearance, the police have no leads. No special identifier has come to the hospital. Her credit card and bank account has not been used. It seems she has simply vanished. To Ishan, Navi was the center of his life and everything to him. His lost was unimaginable. In addition, the community is filled with questions.

Where has Navi Ahuja gone to? Has she been abducted or still alive? As the investigators looks deeper in Navi's disappearance, a strange call makes them question everything they thought they knew about the Christian couple. A phone call came in, a male's voice trying to be disguise, saying, Navi Ahuja was having an affair. Minister Ishan and Navi are community leader in their church, but Navi has vanished without a trace. The police have fast tracked the case. Even though it has been less 48 hours, Navi is officially a missing person. Both Navi's husband and the church are growing more and more concerned, that she may have suffered a terrible misfortune. After Navi's got missing, the police has found their first evidence. The pickup truck she was driving was found not far from her home. It looks like somebody simply park the truck and walks away. The truck was found by the roadside with all the doors locked. Who would have kidnapped somebody, packed the truck by the roadside, and locked the doors. But the truck does provides a valiable piece of evidence to the police. The way the truck was packed, it does not show any sign that somebody was dragged or forced out of the truck. Navi stands only 6 feet 8 inches tall. She would not have needed the seat pushed back if she was driving. It seems likely that a man was driving Navi Ahuja's truck. But who? It could not have been her husband Ishan because he was seen in the community play when Navi vanished. The police quickly eliminated him as a suspect. But they wondered, could this unknown man be a friend? Or even a lover?

Chapter 2

In a community where infidelity is very far away to be mentioned. Therefore, if she were having an affair with somebody else, she would have just picked up and left. The probability becomes more credible when a local mechanic, Nishan Babu, said that he encountered a man on the road where Navi's truck was found on the night of her disappearance. He also said that as he was driving by at that night, he saw a man walking along the road. Then he said to himself that must be the man's truck that was parking by the roadside, maybe it brokedown. He offered to give him a ride, but the man turns his head away quickly from him as if he was trying to avoid him, saying no! no!!, I got it, I got it, everything is fine. But this was a brief encounter and the mechanic cannot offer much description of the man. A large man with dark hair. It could be anyone. The police has followed the little physical evidence available to the and it led to a dead end.

The detectives decided to reinter view Ishan to see if there is anything in the timeline of Navi Ahuja's disappearance might yield a new clue. They wanted to know if they both have been arguing and quarreling. But Ishan said no that they both have been happily married and have no idea why Navi would have gone missing. But weeks have passed and Ishan finally tells the police more. He said to the police that besides appearances, behind closed doors, his marriage has not always been perfect. It is possible that Ishan does not want the police to know the details of their private life, and tried to keep them off believing that it should remain a private matter, and Navi would still return home. The longer the time that she stayed missing, the more he may have felt that he wanted to let the police in so they could help find Navi.

Ishan made an intimate disclosure to the police. He suffers from sexual disfunction. Something that has caused conflict in his marriage with Navi. Moreover, he admits those six years ago, he had sinned with another woman. Actually, nobody really know what goes on in the marriage other than the husband and wife. And I think it is very simple, in fact the husband and wife had given a very solid appearance that they are having a very happy marriage. And in fact behind closed doors it is not the case at all. But Ishan is also adamant that his affair is long over and that they both had put it past them. He also said that when it came to light, he confesses to Navi. She forgave him and they went on with the ministry. Even though she may forgive him, she does not forget. So it is still there. Navi could have thought to herself, will Ishan forgive me for this? He has done it and would have no right no to forgive me. We are forgiven and Christian people. Therefore, she could have been motivated by those ideas and may have had a less than appropriate relationship. Ishan also told the police those three weeks before Navi's disappearance, he received a very strange phone call. He said the phone call was a male's voice, and he was trying to be disguised. The caller said that my wife Navi was having an affair. Even people in the class and very high people can make mistake. So it is possible that she might have a very weak moment, and ran with it. Pastor Ishan have finally given the police some understanding why his wife Navi may have willingly left him. But if Navi had a boyfriend, it was a closely held secret. And no one who knew her could give the police any more information. Detectives most also consider the possibility that Navi was abducted or attacked. But if she was, there is no physical evidence that can lead them to a suspect. The investigation has come to a standstill.

Then in the days and weeks after Navi's disappearance, hope for her return is revived. The police receive multiple reports that she has been spotted in various nearby town. Despite numerous sighting, the police are never able to locate Navi. None of the reports yielded any results. But with the call suggested Navi's affair, and the multiple sightings, evidence is building that perhaps Navi is alive and have left Ishan for another man. Many people get missing because they wanted to go away. Navi could easily have run away. Perhaps she ran away with her love, or she ran away to another town or country, or another life. Under the cloud of Ishan's wife disappearance, Ishan has reluctantly revealed some of the couple's secrets. But there are much darker things still hidden. There is someone who knows much about the police secret. Whenever you bring someone new into your life, that you get to know him in an intimate way, there is always the potential for disaster. Shortly after Navi's disappearance, her husband told the police that because of trouble in their marriage, Novi might have left him for a new love.

As the days passed with no new leads, and no word from Navi, her love ones become more and more desperate for some answers. They know that the longer Navi was missing, the colder the trail to find her grows. Her niece said that she cannot sleep and anytime the phone rings she will just jump. It is almost being a prisoner in your own home. Navi Novi's niece Roja Patel, searches for some answers and she made a very odd discovery. While looking at a website connected to Ishan and Navi's church, she sees a picture of a woman currently on a mission to Croatia. Almost unbelievably, the woman looks exactly like Navi Ahuja. Could Navi must have gone to a mission in Croatia? And if so, why she would not have told anyone. Why would it be such a closely held secret. Navi's niece brings the website to the attention of the authorities. They checked the picture and compared it to the picture of Navi, and said that there was a 99% chance that it could be her on that picture. The members of Navi's church said that they have no knowledge of Navi being in Croatia for a mission. The police decided to dig deeper in the police community looking for clues.

The authority is looking for people that were very close. The investigators were told about one young man who had lived with Ishan and Navi Ahuja. But when they tried to track him down for questioning, they discover that he had suddenly left the country. Although he had scheduled to start studying medicine in the university, the former healthcare of the police decided to deferred his education and go on a mission. The police felt hat does not make any sense. He supposed to go to the university to start studying medicine and suddenly deferred his admission for a missionary work. They later discovered that he had travelled to Bulgaria, a country not far from Croatia, where Navi's is suspected to be. Everyone wants to know what is the relationship between this young man and Navi truly is. Navi's niece, Roja, was suspecting that the young man could be in Croatia with Navi. And the law enforcement are aware that there is a specific reason why Bulgaria may be attractive to some. It is one of the few countries that have no extradiction treaty with India. Some people have committed serious crime and fled to Bulgaria. And because there is no extradiction treaty, they could not be extradicted. The investigators are convinced that this young man is the key to know what happen to Navi. Does he knows where she is? Why did he leave the country so sudden after Navi vanished. The investigators flew to Bulgaria and try to interview him. They felt that there was something he knew they really needed. But when the investigators arrived in Bulgaria, they are told he is not there. He was slipped into Croatia, the very same place the picture on the website suggested Navi's might be.

The investigators tried to track the young man down for months but with no success. Finally, five years after Navi's disappearance, they get a break. The young man voluntarily returned to India. And when the investigators questioned him, and he has a very compelling story to tell. He said de does not know where Navi is, but doubt she would have gone on a mission without telling anyone. He said he and Navi were not romantically involved, and that he does not believe that she would be having an affair with anyone else. Her Christian value simply would not have permitted it. But he also tells the police something else. That, Ishan is not always the good pastor he made himself to be. He said Ishan is cruel and nasty. He often directed most of his cruelty to Navi. The investigators said that anytime they talked to Ishan, he is always meek, humble and gentle. And there is no sign that he is cruel or hash.

Chapter 3

The young man was cleared as a suspect. But the police begin to consider something, that one seem impossible. Could this man called the man of God actually be responsible for his wife's disappearance? The law enforcement takes a deeper look on the who was so devastated when Navi went missing. Who discussed an unsatisfactory sex life with his wife? Who even admitted to a past affair of his own? The revelation that he was not that disciplined man he presented to the community is changing the nature of the investigation. Could he be keeping even darker secret? Somebody who is living a double life. Somebody who is living a lie, and serious interest in keeping his or her secret life secret, like a pastor of a church who is engaging in illicit sex. He may be willing to go to any length not to be caught, to protect that secret and to protect his public face.

Even though there is still no evidence connecting Ishan to the crime, years after his wife's disappearance, Ishan has become personally interested in the case. But it is difficult for investigators to proceed. The police could not get a search warrant because they need a crime to do that. A missing person is not a crime. What really happened to Navi is still a secret, but not for long. One civil engineer Rohan Burman, was doing some work in the bush until his foot steps on something. He picked it up and it was a woman's bra. Five years have past and Navi is still missing. The police suspected her husband the well regarded pastor Ishan was somehow involved. Although it is still hard for many to believe. The community are thinking that it cannot be him. They are thinking that how can it be him. In a case like this where you have such a happily married Christian couple, it will be very difficult to draw to conclusion that Ishan could have been involved in her wife's disappearance. Then five years after her disappearance, a truly terrible discovery is made.

A river just milled where Navi's truck was abandoned, a civil engineer comes across a chilling site. He was narrating his experience to the police. My foot steps on something and I had a crack. I saw bones and bra within the bones. The police immediately went to the scene and discovered the remains of a human being buried on the spot the engineer found the bones and the bra. They found some jewelries and a ring. Then they assumed that it was a female. It also appeared that one of the skeleton's hand has been bound, which led them to believe a foul play. They found a rope that may have been used to restrained something. Or may be have been used to killed someone. The remains were sent to the lab for test. Dental record confirmed the match, that this is Navi Ahuja. Well it is impossible to confirmed the exact time of death. These bones have been here a long time. Very likely Navi was killed the very day her husband reported her gone. There was no longer any doubt, Navi was brutally murdered. All the rumours that she had been in Croatia on a mission has failed, because she is now been found dead in India.

First thing the law enforcement would do when a case changes from missing person to homicide, is to go back to all the evidence that was gathered to try to find who they want to see through the lens of suspect. They went to work on reinter viewing people. The first person the investigators speak to was Ishan, Navi's husband. As Navi's surving husband, the police needs to inform him about Navi's remains. But Ishan reaction to this devastating news is strange. The police have long suspected Ishan in his wife's disappearance. They have no forensic eveidence to tie him to the crime, much less a brutal murder. Ishan is beloved in his community. But now the police know much more about Ishan character. And is hardly for what one would expect from a man of God. The police decides to reinter view previous witnesses.

Looking for information that may have been overlooked the first time around. On top of their list is Nishan Babu, the mechanic, who witnessed a mysterious man walking on the road near Navi's truck, on the night of the disappearance. Ishan was not a suspect at the time. But after the police showed the mechanic Ishan's photograph, he was percent sure that he was the man he saw that night walking on the road near Navi's truck, the night of her disappearance. The police now have a witness that places Ishan at the scene of Navi's disappearance. The investigators now decided to dig deeper into the personal and financial records of Ishan and Navi. They knew that a paper trail can lead to a place where some people deeper secret can be found.

There were two credit cards there that were overdue. So it shows a different picture that everything was not as wonderful as it appeared or portrayed to be. But they have a serious financial difficulties. But Ishan and Navi did not live an extravagant life style. And Navi even took an extra work to give them a financial cushion. Why could not they afford topay their bills. Has Ishan started another affair? Or was he spending money on a new lover? Or was it a different kind of secret entirely? Her niece said that, Navi never told them anything, and they never suspected that anything is going wrong because Navi never complained. She kept everything to her self. The police is about to discover that the devoted minister had a secret that no one who knew him could ever have imagined. After the remains of Navi was found, a witnessed has identified Ishan as the man he saw walking on the road near Navi's truck the night of her disappearance. Wasds it possible this man of God has killed his wife?

New clues point in that direction. When reexamine all the evidence in the case file, detectives came across photos of Ishan taken the day of the first investigation. The first thing they saw was scratches on the left side of his face. At that time, Ishan has an easy explanation of the mark on his face. He said he fell on the bars, and that is how he got those scratches on his face. In the day immediately after his wife's disappearance, the soft spoken pastor was not considered as a suspect in he case. And Navi was a missing person and not a murder victim. But is now cleared that Navi was violently murdered. Those scratches looks very very bad for Ishan. Also those marks on his face tells you that they do not comes from bars. The police took the photograph to a forensic pathologist, who stated that the scratches could have been made by a human fingernail. Whatever doubt the investigators have about Ishan's guilt are quickly fading. They think that they have stumble on physical clues that the minister killed his wife. Navi has told the police who killed her by the marks she left on her husband's face. But the investigators needs more evidence if they are going to convict Ishan. They cannot go into court with an expert theory about photographs that are five years old. Then going through the couples bank records and phone bills, they found something odd.

A call to one number over and over again. Numerous times a week. The charges is nearly 100,000 thousand Rupees in a single month. The numbers was a sex hotline. Ishan has an obsession of making phone sex calls. He was calling other ladies and really liked to call them. Ishan has been running massive phone bills by calling sex hotlines. The well respected pastor was addicted to a fantasy world. Where he paid real money at an exorbitant rate to any woman to fulfil his fantacies. He does not have a self esteem and the phone sex is giving him a really self esteem. The police determine that Ishan is addicted to phone sex. It is hardly a secret a religious leader would want people to know. The police also thinks that Navi did know about the phone sex her husband is doing and thousands of rupees he is spending on the phone sex was bankrupting their house hold.

Navi did not like the way Ishan was spending the money, because she was working very hard for it. Ishan has a sex problem, calling telephone lines for sex ladies. He has deceived everyone, and counselling his congregation to do good. But he was living with a lie all the time. The police also soon learned that Ishan was running on debt on the church credit card, perhaps due to its sex calls. It is obvious that this fetish and what Ishan has spent on it will be massive scandal on their church and community if it got out. Ishan motive for murder becomes abundantly clear. He is an important member of the church so it matters. He cannot do this. He knows he cannot do it. But he cannot control it. Ishan finally lose everything. His church, his followers and most importantly his Christian image if Navi reveals his secrets. The secrets she knew about Ishan is big and can destroy his integrity. His behaviors, his habits and if she ever talked it, it will destroy him and the church community. And that was what they basically lived for, the church community.

It would have been so humiliating for him. Ishan was willing to kill his wife, his life partner to protect himself. Investigators learned that the day before her disappearance, Navi has bounced her chair. It seems possible that small incident could have triggered that deadly argument between the two, because Navi saw the latest phone call bills and urged Ishan to make a confession of what is happening. The reason being that the cheque Navi took to the bank got bounced back because there was no more money in their bank account. She came home and got it hot with Ishan. That cheque was the straw that broke the camel's back. Therefore, she got fed up and made her mind that she was going to leave Ishan. The whole situation really got out of control. Ishan needed Navi to bring more money, but she refused. Ishan believes he did not do anything wrong. He believes that his needs are far more important than Navi. He wanted his secrets to remain secret and that the community should see him on who he wanted them to believe. So he did not want Navi to leave. Nearly five years after Navi's death, the police has finally put the pieces together to find out what happened. Most likely, Navi confronted Ishan over his phone sex addiction. She may have threatened to reveals his secrets and shame him before the church community if he did not stop.

The police believe when their argument got out of control, Ishan strangled Navi inside their house. After dumping her body inside the bush, he abandoned her truck by the side of the road, and went home, encountering the mechanic on the way. It would be over five years Navi's bones will be discovered by a civil engineer. The district Attorney, Tashi Agarwal, takes this theory to the jury, along with the mechanic testimony, that Ishan was the man he saw on the road that night. After three hours of deliberation, they found Ishan Ahuja, guilty of murder. He is sentenced to life in prison. Ishan killed his wife to cover up his secret phone sex addiction. And he almost got away with. If Navi remains have not been found, this case could still be opened. There will still be a missing person report case.

Dark Heart

Chapter 1

June 2000, a woman sets off from her Makati home, in Manila, the Philippines, to spend the weekend with her ex-boyfriend and his daughter in Novatos, Manila, Philippines. She is never seen again. The woman is Alexa Flores, a 42 year old writer and illustrator, with a sense of humour. She started writing her first book when she was in the university. She made pictures using dots from her pencil. She was writing for a children's magazine, and she was also working for children, making children participating in art works. Alexa is a woman with many friends, and many persons. Alexa is famous in her dance class. She was a very beautiful woman and very intelligent. She is someone who was very vital, educated and artistic. Alexa life is very full and over the years there is one thing she has always long for. She wants a profound and successful relationship. When she met Joshua Lopez, Alexa felt she has finally found an enduring love. They all lived in Manila city, the Philippines.

Manila, is the capital of the Philippines and one of the municipalities that comprise Metro Manila. The city is located on the eastern shore of Manila Bay on Luzon, the country's largest island. Manila is the hub the Metro Manila area, also known as the National Capital Region (NCR), a thriving metropolitan area consisting of seventeen cities and municipalities which is home to over 10 million people. Manila is the second most populous city proper in the Philippines, with more than 1.5 million inhabitants. Only nearby Quezon City, the country's former capital, is more populous.

The name Manila comes from may nilad, Tagalog for "there is nilad," referring to the flowering mangrove plant that grew on the marshy shores of the bay. In the sixteenth century, Manila (then Maynilad) grew from an Islamic settlement on the banks of the Pasig River into the seat of the colonial government of Spain when it controlled the Philippine Islands for over three centuries from 1565 to 1898. After the end of the Spanish-American War in 1898, the United States occupied and controlled the city and the Philippine archipelago until 1946. During World War II, much of the city was destroyed. The Metropolitan Manila region was enacted as an independent entity in 1975. Today, the city and the metropolis thrive as an important cultural and economic center. However, overpopulation, traffic congestion, pollution, and crime challenge the city. Intramuros, or the 'Walled City', is one of the oldest districts of Manila, built on the south bank of the Pasig River around 1571. It was built by the Spaniards – more specifically by Miguel Lopez de Legaspi – and is bound on all sides by moats and thick, high walls, with some over 6 meters high.

While the district was originally home to an Indianized-Malayan-Islamic settlement, it became the centre of religious, political and military power in the 16th century, when the country was under the control of Spain. Only the elite Spaniards and Mestizos were allowed accommodation in Intramuros. That is obviously not the case now, but the historic buildings and features remain as testament to the Philippines' challenging past. Divisoria Market is crowded and chaotic, but with lots of opportunities for a good bargain. Located in the middle of Chinatown in Manila, it's famous for its street stalls that sell just about anything, from clothes, bags, textiles, accessories and electronics to religious items, pirated DVDs, household and office supplies, fruits and vegetables, and toys. You will see a lot of knock-off products, but if you keep your eyes peeled, there are some really good finds here.

The market is famous for its retail and wholesale shops. For those who do not fancy shopping out in the streets, there are air-conditioned malls that house hundreds of these bargain stalls. It can be a maze inside so, if you spot something you like, go ahead and buy it right away or write down the stall number in case you decide to go back for it. Haggling is expected here, so do not be shy and give it your best shot. Typically, you will get a really good discount if you buy in bulk (about 5 to 6 pieces of the same item). Divisoria Market is not for those who hate crowds and busy streets. However, if you are up for a real shopping adventure, put on a comfortable pair of shoes and have fun. It is a popular shopping destination for many Filipinos, but you'll also spot tourists looking around for souvenirs to bring back home. Like in any crowded places, beware of pickpockets. We recommend shopping here on weekday mornings, when the crowds are at its thinnest.

Fort Santiago is a 16th-century citadel, a national landmark and a shrine to the hard-won freedom of the Philippines. It's been a cornerstone of the country's history, seeing the defeat of Rajah Sulayman the Spaniards, the invasion of the Chinese led by Limahong, and the first raising of the US flag that declared the beginning of American rule. The solid stone structure has an Italian-Spanish architectural style. Miguel Lopez de Legaspi built the fort for the newly established Manila City and named it after Spain's patron saint – St. James the Great. It is also known as Fuerza de Santiago in Spanish or Moog ng Santiago in Tagalog. Right by the Pasig River and containing the green Plaza de Armas, Fort Santiago is a great spot for family picnics and other open-air activities. But if you're visiting for the history, you certainly won't be disappointed. The fort served as a prison for national hero Jose Rizal before his execution in 1896. The Jose Rizal Museum was set up to display related memorabilia and to honour this great man. To commemorate the final walk from his cell to the firing squad, his footsteps have been embedded onto the ground in bronze. Another feature worth checking out is a white cross that commemorates the bravery of the freedom fighters who were imprisoned in the dungeons here.

Fort Santiago forms one corner of the walled city of Intramuros and is a great source of history, showcasing historical remains such as cannons, ammunition, soldiers' quarters, a canal and other memorabilia. :20You will also find modern amenities like theatre houses, restaurants, souvenir shops and refreshment stands. San Agustin Church in Manila should be on the itinerary of anyone with an interest in history or architecture. Located inside the historic Walled City of Intramuros, this Roman Catholic Baroque-style church is a UNESCO World Heritage site.

Built by the Spaniards in the 16th century, the church has survived a major earthquake in 1863 as well as the ravages of World War II. You cannot miss this church when you are out and about in Intramuros, but we recommend booking a tour through your hotel. The San

Agustin Church also features an impressive museum, which will give you an idea of just how deep the Catholic faith runs throughout this country. There is an admission fee, but it is well worth it. The museum's galleries display the works of the Augustinian monks in the Philippines and are divided into several categories, including love of nature, science, and more. Unsurprisingly, many of the artefacts have a religious theme. There are stunning frescoes, the Trompe-l'oeil ceiling, paintings, statues, and various church ornaments, all of which you can appreciate with a background of pipe organ music. If you are planning to visit the San Agustin Church, it's worth knowing that it's a popular wedding venue. While it is interesting to witness a Filipino wedding, access to the church is restricted during the ceremony.

For just over a year, they have been living together. On June 13, 2000, the day after Alexa set out for weekend in the Novatos city, Joshua Lopez gets a phone call. He learned Alexa did not show up in her ex-boyfriend's house. Joshua files a missing person report and speaks to the media. Sergeant Bayani Perez takes on the case of Alexa Flores. Joshua Lopez told the police what he has been doing Friday evening, barely him and Alexa went out to rent a movie. He told the police that Carlo Ramos who is Alexa's boyfriend in the past, called the house and Alexa talked to him for about an hour. Alexa had maintained a friendship with her ex-boyfriend Carlo Ramos and his young daughter who was celebrating her birthday that weekend. Saturday morning, they woke up, lay the bed, and discussed the plan for the day. From that point, she told Joshua that she was going to visit Carlo Ramos. She packs her bags and left between one and 1:15. That was the last time he saw her until he received a phone call Sunday afternoon. Joshua calls another friend Cherry Tan, who lives in the area. She discovered Alexa jeep at the side of the road, not too far from Carlo Ramos cottage.

Cherry also said that there is no sign of anything. The doors of the jeep were locked and inside Alexa bags was at the back of the jeep and her purse in the front. With the help of Joshua and others close to Alexa, the police search the area where the vehicle was found. But there was no trace of Alexa, in the bushes and the river. Joshua kept searching in his own initiative. Joshua is making up posters, standing by the road side showing it and talking to each person driving on the road. He is all there all the time searching for Alexa. Sergeant Bayani Perez was determine to find Alexa dead or alive. In June 13, 2000, writer and justice advocate Alexa Flores, leaves her Makati home for a weekend visit to her ex-boyfriend and his young daughter. Alexa Flores never arrived. Her jeep is found an hour North of the city of Novatos. It is locked with all her belongings in it. Her new husband Joshua Lopez, joined the police to search the area. But there is no trace of Alexa.

As the police dog deeper into Alexa's disappearance, sergeant Bayani takes a statement from Joshua and learnt from the unusual way he met Alexa. Sergeant Bayani just continue talking to Joshua and got to know a bit about him, and he was quite true with information. The couple met at the supreme court hearing, into the most notorious case of the wrongfully imprisonment the Philippine history, the case of Paolo Sanchez. Alexa was doing a book on Sanchez because she wanted to write a book on Paolo. Joshua came forward voluntarily to identify already convicted felon, Manny Manalo. He is the man who committed the crime for which Paolo Sanchez has unjustly been convicted. But at the time, Joshua was a convict himself. Due to Joshua courageous actions, Alexa fell for him.

Alexa began writing to Joshua, and within a short time they were romantically involved. And she was working to get him an early parole. The grew and involved, and it developed into a plan to get him out of jail, so that he can put out a life with her. Sergeant Bayani, wants to know more about the life of Joshua criminal past and Joshua is surprisingly frank. Joshua said to him that he killed somebody in 1975. Joshua had been convicted for manslaughter for killing a woman in a hotel. That was 15 years before and Joshua was high on cocaine. Sergeant Bayani saw him as a man who deserve a second chance. Alexa saw Joshua as a man who lived a hard life. She thinks he has been abused physically. He was into drugs and she wanted to be that one woman who will make a difference in his life. Sergeant Bayani also thinks that Joshua deserves some benefits of the doubt. But that he has to be very open minded. They have to give some credit to Joshua because he reported Alexa Flores missing.

Chapter 2

In their time together, Alexa have given Joshua unflagging support. She set him up a business model and bought him some tools for doing gardening and land scraping business. Joshua said that although he had a criminal history but he will never do anything to harm Alexa.. In her home in the Novatos, Angela Garcia, the private detective is closely observing the unfolding drama. Angela is keeping an opened mind and wanted to help Joshua find Alexa. She is feeling sorry for him. She is also feeling sorry for Alexa that disappeared. Angela who moved to the Philippines from her native England, three years before, is just completing a training about a private eye. This case is playing out just as she is looking for a practical one. Angela said that where Alexa's jeep was found was 30 minutes from where she lives, and that makes her uncomfortable. She calls to volunteer her assistance to Alexa distress partner, Joshua Lopez. Angela is nervous, but she is also driven by strong personal motivation and to help Alexa, as she believes she had to start with Joshua.

In Joshua's house, Angela ask if she can take the conversation, and Joshua is entirely comfortable. After the conversation with Joshua, Angela goes to the site where Alexa abandoned jeep was found, not far from the cottage of her ex-boyfriend Carlo Ramos. Inside the jeep was found Alexa's belongings including gift for Carlo Ramos daughter for her birthday. She took a walk to the cottage and there was nobody there. In late June, many local cottages are still closed up. Angela wondered what could have happened to Alexa in this lonely country side. Joshua criminal past has made him a suspect for Alexa's disappearance. But the police do not want to jump into conclusion. It seems Joshua has no motive for killing Alexa. Sergeant Bayani wants to know more about Carlo Ramos, the ex-boyfriend that Alexa was planning to visit. Carlo Ramos and Alexa Flores has been on and on relationship. Ramos left Alexa when she was with Joshua. Was Ramos jealous that Alexa left him for Joshua?

Joshua used to think that Ramos is the prime suspect. He confines his suspicions to the private investigator Angela Garcia over a number of meetings. According to Angela, Joshua was thinking due to the abusive relationship Ramos had with Alexa, he could have something to do with Alexa's disappearance. Sergeant Bayani paid a visit to Carlo Ramos at his work place at the university of Manila. He gives the detective an alibi. Ramos said that he spent the whole weekend at the cottage with his daughter. Due to the fact that Alexa's vehicle was not far from Ramos house, the police stage another search. This time on Ramos land. But there is no trace of Alexa. And no evidence to implicate Carlo Ramos. Bayani considers that if there could be anyone else who can have a motive for harming Alexa. Joshua was also suspecting Manny Manlo, because he testified against him in court, on behalf of Paolo Sanchez. Joshua claimed Manalo had threatened him before.

At the time of Alexa's disappearance, Manalo was out of prison. He has not yet been charged for the murder Paolo Sanchez has served time for. May be Manalo wanted to punish Joshua by kidnapping and killing Alexa. The detective is looking into the where about of Manny Manalo. By June 22, about 7:15 in the morning, Manny Manalo was arrested and taking into custody by the police. It also happened that Alexa Flores got missing on that same day. So Manalo was eliminated as a suspect. Meanwhile, in Novatos, Angela is looking for new insight into the case, by playing back the tape he made with conversation with Alexa's partner, Joshua Lopez. Joshua had had inspected Alexa's jeep after it was found. That is where she heard something that blind sight her. According to the tape, Joshua said, this is exactly the way I left it, and again he changed his statement and said, no, I mean it is exactly the way Alexa left it. Could this be a simple slip of the tongue? Or could it be that the man she has befriended and volunteered to help is in fact Alexa murderer?

In 2000, writer, illustrator and justice advocate Alexa Flores leaves her Makati home and disappears. Her husband Joshua Lopez, had been convicted of manslaughter for the death of a woman 15 years earlier. But he has won Alexa's trust through his testimony in a high profile case wrongfully imprisonment. And it seems he is shattered by Alexa's disappearance. Angela Garcia who had volunteered to help find Alexa is picked by an inseminating slip he made in their tape conversation about Alexa's jeep. Angela wonders if Joshua is in fact responsible for Alexa's disappearance. As for the police, after the investigation of two other suspects goes no where, then they started focusing their attention on Joshua. They learnt that Joshua owed Alexa over $20,000. It was just at that point she disappeared. Sergeant Bayani paid a visit to the bank manager Nicole Valdez, who said that Alexa was increasingly agitated by Joshua failure to repay her. Valdez said Alexa and Joshua financial problem went beyond paid loan. Joshua has being withdrawing money from Alexa's bank account and depositing in his own bank account by forging her signature on her cheque.

And when Alexa finds out she would be blaming the bank that it was their mistake, because she never made such transactions. The bank investigated the matter and later discovered that it was Joshua who was actually doing the illegal bank transactions. Sergeant Bayani can now see a motive for Joshua Lopez. Bayani said that Alexa was probably going to turn Joshua to the police about what has been going on regarding the illegal bank transactions made on her bank account by Joshua Lopez. Bayani then questioned Valdez about any banking transaction made on the day of Alexa's disappearance. He made a straggling discovery. When Joshua first reports Alexa is missing, he said she left Makati at 1:20 pm. When Alexa's jeep was found, her bank card was in it. On 2:55pm, June 22, the bank card was used to withdraw $280. The bank surveillance tape reveals it was Joshua who used Alexa's bank credit card at the time Alexa was supposedly out of town. Technology caught him on the line. Joshua Lopez is officially the prime suspect. According to forensic behavior specialist, DR Dennis Gonzales, Joshua displays a number of psychopathic characteristics. A psychopath is the ultimate body pressure. That is where the conning, manipulation, and the word charming which comes up with a lot of people being in relationship with a psychopath. You will here words like, charming; he was so charming. Bayani said that Joshua is extremely smooth like you will say a real good conned man.

Chapter 3

Before Bayani can convict this killer, he knows he needs more evidence. Bayani confrs in the prosecutor's office. The prosecutor said that without Alexa's body it will be very difficult to convict Joshua on murder charges. And that they need to find that body. The police bugged Joshua's house, and a surveillance is set up to watch the premises. The police discovered that Joshua was having a conversation with someone called Angela Garcia. He seems to like her. He was telling her a lot of information. That if she believed him and helped him out, she would add credibility to his story. When the police realized that Angela is a private investigator, the decided she could be a huge asset to the case. The police told her that they want to talk to her on the case that she was on. First they need to know what she thinks about Joshua Lopez and Alexa Flores. She replied, I think Joshua Killed her. Then the police makes an exceptional request. When the police discovered that Angela has gained his trust, they ask her to work with them to help close the net on Joshua. Angela has made a big promise to sergeant Bayani.

Getting the body is crucial to the case of Joshua Lopez. To find the body, Angela the private investigator made a plan. While the police listen in, Angela turns the table on Joshua as she uses his attempt to cast blame on Alexa's ex-boyfriend against him. The police wants Angela to play along with it. According to Dennis Gonzales, an expert in psycho pathology, the strategy could work. Angela urges Joshua to with her to the woods to search for Alexa. So Joshua gave her a day they could go and search for Alexa in the woods. The police would do everything they can to ensure her safety. On a sweltering July day, Angela drives into the Novatos hills with a man who is a convicted killer. The police had two surveillance team out there totaling covering her. But on a quiet country roads, surveillance team cannot follow too closely.

They finally got there and went for a walk through the woods. It is the early summer 2000, and Angela is in the woods searching for the body of Alexa Flores. A woman who has been missing and presumed dead, for just over two months. Angela was accompany by Joshua Lopez, Alexa's ex-husband, who is now suspected to be her killer. In the public eye, he has played the role of a grieving spouse. And Angela have come forward to volunteered her help for him in finding Alexa. But Joshua Lopez did not know that now Angela is working with the Makati police. If he realizes, Angela could be in grave danger. A surveillance team is tracking every move of Angela's journey. That is, until they lose sight of she and Joshua and what could be a crucial moment. The surveillance team can hear everything but they have no idea in the woods where they are. Everywhere were so quiet in the woods.

Suddenly the quiet was broken by a helicopter. Her safety were the primary concern the police had. The police was relieved to see that she is safe, but the operation could be blown due to the police helicopter patrolling the sky over the woods. Joshua then asked Angela if she was an undercover. Angela raised her too hands up and said, you can search me. The Joshua said, no I am not going to do that. But Joshua aborted the search. For weeks after Joshua refused to go back to look for Alexa's body, Angela and Sergeant Bayani devised a plan to motivate Joshua, using Alexa's money as a bate. The police had called Nicole Valdez, the bank manager, to let Joshua knows the rules of getting access to Alexa's bank account. Joshua is the heir to Alexa's estate. But Valdez tells him that until her body is found, Alexa cannot be declared dead, and he cannot inherit her money. Joshua has no money at all, no money to pay the bills. He does not have any access to any money. Joshua was taking properties in their house such as computers, printers and many more things to the pawn shop to exchange for money.

The next component of the plan is to make Joshua believes that the police are hovering on Carlo Ramos as the prime suspect. Joshua was with Angela in a bar drinking beer, discussing and having a good time. The police who are watching them was not comfortable with the scene as they are more concern about the safety of Angela. And with good reason according to criminal psychologist, DR Dennis

Gonzales, the game should go on as planned, though it is very risky. Suddenly, Angela got a call on her phone, and it was the police telling her to get out of there. She pretends to talking to her daughter. She then told Joshua that she have to go home to see her daughter until the next day, and Joshua agreed. Angela has accomplished what she sets out to do. But the police was hard on her. They said she cannot get so close to Joshua because he is too dangerous. The police were thinking that Angela had some feelings about Joshua because of the kisses they had in the bar. But Angela said she had to play that role because Joshua was suspecting her to be an undercover. She is still desperate on finding Alexa's body. The police should believe and trust in her. The police and Angela are suspecting that Alexa's body is hidden deep in the forest. Angela is now convinced that it was Joshua who killed his common law wife, Alexa Flores.

And she had been working with the police to entrap him. Joshua is convinced that finding the body will lead to the arrest of Alexa ex-boyfriend Carlo Ramos, by this he will be allowed to claim Alexa's money and estate. In fact, the police are poised to charge Joshua. They are depending on the recovery of the body for the evidence they need. If Angela loses Joshua's trust, a killer could get away with murder. Even worse, Angela could be his next victim. On July 14, 2000, Angela drives to the woods with Joshua, for the second time. Joshua may be weary of a trap, but criminal psychologist DR Dennis Gonzales, comments on why he might be compel to return to the woods. The police had wired Angela's purse for sound, and she tries to keep them abreast of their where about. Angela returns to the place she enters the woods with Alexa's killer. It seems Joshua is not so much searching as he is leading Angela. Then Joshua said to Angela, as they walk in the woods, just be careful, there must be barbwire. Then Angela replied, how did you know there is barbwire? But Joshua did not say anything to that. Then as they come upon a clearing, something catches Angela's eye. She found Alexa's shoes on the ground. Joshua became very nervous and was steering at Angela.

Angela too became scared, but she summoned up courage. She went to Joshua and held him saying, Joshua, we have found her, it is ok, and it is ok. You are going to be all right. At that point, Joshua blinks his eyes and Angela felt safe. If she had not acted that way, she could have been Joshua's next victim. She was very convincing, knowing what to say to calm him down. The Joshua went on his knees and cried, Alexa!, Alexa!!, Alexa!!!. The surveillance team have heard everything. Later that afternoon when they have left the woods, Joshua reports the discovery of the body to the police. He is confident that the murder will be pinned on Carlo Ramos. But instead, Joshua was confronted by the police and arrested. The moment Joshua walked into the police station for questioning, he never saw freedom again. Joshua Lopez is found guilty of first degree murder, though he maintained his innocence. Joshua Lopez strangled Alexa in the bath tub and killed her. Then he wrapped her body, put it in the back of her jeep and took her off. He then deposited her dead body in a bunch of bushes inside the woods. and cover her up. The police suspected Joshua Lopez is responsible for the unsolved murder of two additional women. But within two months of sentencing, he dies from Hepatitis C.

The Accountant

Chapter 1

In the spring of 1985, Bao and Chau Pham, seems to fulfil a life long dream. For years their small jewelry company Bando Jewelry, have been struggling with its day-to-day earnings. But recently, Bando Jewelry is suddenly flooded with cash. The hardworking couple has finally made it big. The company that has been doing one million dollars a year business suddenly grew to 5 million dollars a year business. Bao and Chau have been married for over 10 years. And nearly all that time together have been trying to make Bando Jewelry into a success. Now they are enjoying the fruits of their labour. They bought a new house in Hanoi. They have very beautiful Jewelries and took lavish vacations. Although, the couple is reaping the reward of their success, the clue of Bando Jewelry sudden turn around, does not rest exclusively with them. The company financial accountant, seems to accelerate with the arrival of a skilled new book keeper. Bao and Chau Pham both live and do business in Hanoi, the Vietnam capital city.

Hanoi is Vietnam's capital city. It is the political hub of the country, as well as the cultural and historical center. Founded more than 1,000 years ago, the city remains steeped in tradition. Hanoi was occupied by the Chinese for much of its early history, and later by the French. Both countries left a lasting cultural imprint. Centuries-old Buddhist temples are scattered throughout the city, often set alongside hundred-year-old French colonial mansions and an ever-increasing number of modern skyscrapers. It's an eclectic mix of East and West, old and new. Numerous parks and lakes provide shade and tranquility to this otherwise bustling metropolis, as millions of motorbikes, cars, bicycles, buses, and pedestrians all compete for space on roads that weren't originally designed for motorized traffic. Cyclos (three-wheeled pedicabs) sedately ferry wide-eyed tourists through the atmospheric warren of ancient streets. Entire neighborhoods are hidden in the interior of city blocks, accessed by narrow alleys designed only for two-wheeled vehicles and foot traffic.

Beautiful Hoan Kiem Lake is the heart of central Hanoi. This peaceful oasis is surrounded by lovely shade trees and flowers, views of ancient temples, colonial mansions, and the ancient, bustling maze of little streets known as the Old Quarter. In the early morning hours, ladies practice tai-chi by the lake, as the men huddle together playing Chinese chess and gossiping. In the evenings the park comes alive with walkers, joggers, and snuggling lovers. On the weekends, the roads around the lake are closed to motorized traffic, and the entire area transforms into a pedestrian mall, with musicians, artists, happy families, and curious tourists taking over the busy streets. Wherever you live in Hanoi, you will find an eclectic, chaotic hodgepodge of activity that never seems to slow down. Bustling markets, bicycle vendors hawking their products, people whiling away the hours in outdoor beer halls and sidewalk cafés, and children playing in the streets as their mother's chase after them with bowls of food—it's all part of the unique Hanoi experience.

Hanoi is a delightfully livable city due to its unique culture, proximity to many of Vietnam's most impressive tourist attractions, and its low cost of living. There is unique architecture, fascinating historical sites, and a vibrant, traditional city center. Its charming lakes, parks, and tree-lined boulevards are oases of calm in this burgeoning, bustling city. The hot summers, chilly winters, and near-perfect spring and fall weather are an added benefit. It isn't hard to imagine the Hanoi of times past while walking in the warren of small streets and tiny alleyways that make up the Old Quarter. Tiny mom-and-pop shops and a never-ending procession of street vendors sell everything from fruits and vegetables to shoes, flowers, and brooms. Enterprising ladies set up portable kitchens and tiny plastic chairs along the sidewalks, treating diners to fresh, inexpensive meals, using family recipes that have been handed down for generations.

Take a step back in time to Paris in the early 20th century while exploring the French Quarter. Grand French colonial mansions house government buildings, museums, embassies, upscale hotels, and gourmet restaurants. Century-old shade trees provide pleasant respite, near trendy bistros selling fresh pastries, cakes, and strong coffee. Hanoi makes a perfect base to explore many of Vietnam's top attractions. Ba Vi National Park, Cuc Phuong National Park, the UNESCO World Heritage Site of Halong Bay, the exotic Perfume Pagoda, ancient handicraft villages, and the rivers, caves, and mountains of Ninh Binh Province are all easy daytrips from the city.

Hanoi has one of the lowest costs of living of any major city in Southeast Asia. A bag of fresh local vegetables and tropical fruit will not cost more than a couple of dollars at one of the many traditional markets, and supermarkets offer wide selections of local and imported goods at reasonable prices. There are at least two dozen specialty imported food stores in the city and an ever-expanding assortment of restaurants serving international fare—impressive for a city where you couldn't find a hamburger at any price just 10 years ago. Buses transport those who do not want to contend with the traffic, and the fare to practically anywhere in the city is less than 35 cents. Affordable metered taxis are everywhere. A couple can live a comfortable middle-class lifestyle in Hanoi on a budget of $1,000 per month or less.

Hanoi is a favorite traveler's destination due to its unique culture, its proximity to many of Vietnam's most impressive tourist spots, and its low cost of living. There's unique architecture, fascinating historical sites, and a vibrant, traditional city center. Its charming lakes, parks, and tree-lined boulevards are oases of calm in this burgeoning, bustling city. The hot summers, chilly winters, and near-perfect spring and fall weather are also attractive to many foreigners. Hanoi, Vietnam's capital and the second largest city, celebrated its 1,000-year anniversary in 2010. Hanoi has retained many of its ancient traditions, while offering all the modern amenities that expats desire.

It isn't hard to imagine the Hanoi of times past while walking in the warren of small streets and tiny alleyways that make up the Old Quarter. Tiny mom-and-pop shops and a never-ending procession of street vendors sell everything from fruits and vegetables to shoes, flowers, and brooms. Enterprising ladies set up portable kitchens and tiny plastic chairs along the sidewalks, treating diners to fresh, inexpensive meals, using family recipes that have been handed down for generations. Step back in time to Paris in the early 20th century while exploring the French Quarter. Grand French colonial mansions house government buildings, museums, embassies, upscale hotels, and fancy restaurants. Numerous parks and shade trees provide pleasant respite, near trendy bistros selling fresh pastries, cakes, and strong coffee. Central to both the Old Quarter and the French Quarter is peaceful Hoan Kiem Lake, the spiritual heart of Hanoi. Many foreigners have chosen to live in this vibrant part of the city, which is within walking distance of many of Hanoi's finest restaurants, an active nightlife scene, and many of the city's top attractions.

Tay Ho (West Lake) is the largest lake in Hanoi, and Tay Ho District is one of the most popular areas for expats. Restaurants in Tay Ho offer a wide variety of cuisines, ranging from American to Ukrainian, and everything in between. Many shops here sell imported foods and products. Tay Ho is a popular area for expat get-togethers, as only a few tourists venture into this part of the city. Tay Ho is the most expensive district in Hanoi. Many homes are on quiet streets with small yards, and families with children will be close to several well-regarded international schools. The better apartments offer spectacular views overlooking the lake and the city skyline. Retirees who want to live in luxury will often find themselves settling here, though it's possible to find more affordable housing in this area, too. Ba Dinh District is not far from either West Lake or Hoan Kiem Lake, and is the home of many of Hanoi's embassies and administrative buildings. Some of Hanoi's most elegant mansions are located here. Ba Dinh is convenient to both Hoan Kiem and Tay Ho, yet it has a local feel. Foreigners who like the idea of integrating into Vietnamese culture will enjoy living in this part of the city.

There are several large, modern supermarkets, department stores, and malls located in Hanoi. The traditional markets, where fruit, produce, and meat are sold, often offer fresher and less expensive fare than what is found in the supermarkets. Hanoi's JCI accredited Vinmec International Hospital offers comprehensive medical services at reasonable prices. A visit to an English-speaking specialist costs about $30. Several other international hospitals and clinics provide good care to foreigners, though they are often more costly. Many of

Vietnam's top attractions are located within a few hours of Hanoi, including nearby Ba Vi National Park, Cuc Phuong National Park, the UNESCO World Heritage Site of Halong Bay, the exotic Perfume Pagoda, and the rivers, caves, and mountains in Ninh Binh Province. Hanoi is a densely populated city of over 8 million, so few places come with pools or tennis courts—space is always at a premium. If I did want to enjoy those activities, however, I could walk to a hotel in ten minutes and pay a nominal fee for the use of their facilities. Hanoi, Vietnam's bustling capital city, has long been a favorite destination for foreigners. The eclectic mix of architecture is stunning, the food is healthy and delicious, the cost of living is low, and the surrounding area beckons exploration. Most importantly, Hanoians are a welcoming people, and making local friends is easy. Over 10,000 foreigners, myself included, have chosen to make Hanoi their home.

Many foreigners have settled in the Tay Ho (West Lake) district, northwest of the city center, though you will find expats living throughout Hanoi. Tay Ho is full of expat-welcoming restaurants, bars, and shops. Many foreigners who live here teach at one of several international schools in Tay Ho; for the most part, they tend to be younger and more transient than you will find elsewhere in the city. Some older expats also enjoy this part of town, since there are so many places to eat, shop, and meet other like-minded folks. Hanoi has a different expat community than you will find in many other towns with a large population of foreigners, in that, so many of them socialize predominately with the local people. Tay Ho is as close to an enclave as Hanoi gets and even it has a significantly mixed population. There are certainly opportunities for meeting other foreigners, but it seems that many older expats spend more time in the company of local Vietnamese residents, especially once they become comfortable in their newly adopted city. Therefore, so many of Hanoi's older and retired expats live in districts outside of Tay Ho, including the Old Quarter, the French Quarter, and in the part of Ba Dinh District that's near many of the city's embassies. Wherever they live, though, almost everyone takes at least the occasional trip to Tay Ho to buy hard-to-find imported goods, or to take in the outstanding food and nightlife scene in this area.

Chapter 2

Tay Ho's main business district is built along Xuan Dieu Street. From the moment you turn off the Au Co Highway, you'll see evidence of its strong expat influence—L's Place, a supermarket selling mostly imported food, is on the left, and Friend's Bar is on the right. Continue past coffee shops, bars, bakeries, craft beer hangouts, and restaurants catering to an array of nationalities until you get to the Syrena Shopping Center on the left. This mall is not a large one, but it is well tailored to Hanoi's expats. You'll find the Elite Spa and Fitness Center, a large, expat-friendly supermarket, several restaurants specializing in everything from pizza to sushi and ramen, coffee shops, and the excellent (if expensive) Annam Gourmet store, with its huge selection of imported specialty foods, cheeses, sausages, and deli items. As you continue down Xuan Dieu Street, you will see a few streets off to the left; all of them have expat-popular restaurants, coffee shops, fitness centers, spas, and opportunities for nightlife. Pick one you like and visit a few times; before long, you will be a familiar face and making friends will come naturally.

A few places, in particular, are quite popular with Hanoi's expats, and most of them are in Tay Ho. Joma Bakery Café is a long-standing favorite in the heart of the expat neighborhood; they have strong internet and a comfortable area to relax while savoring good coffee, smoothies, pastries, bagels, and light meals. The Moose and Roo Pub and Grill is another place that expats gather to drink and eat; the Canadian owner is a superb host and the North American cuisine is as good as you would find "back home." 7Bridges Hanoi Taproom is a popular place along Xuan Dieu for craft beer and innovative pub food; it's near Tracy's Sports Pub and Burger, a tiny restaurant that serves up great hamburgers in a collegial setting. Texan-owned Anita's Cantina attracts expats who need a good Mexican food fix and a cold margarita; it's usually full every night. There are many other excellent places to eat, drink, and meet others in Tay Ho, with more establishing themselves all the time.

Though you'll find the largest concentration of expat hangouts in Tay Ho, there are many excellent choices in Hanoi's other districts, as well. The Moose and Roo Smokehouse, under the same ownership as the Moose and Roo Pub and Grill in Tay Ho, shares space with the American Club in Hoan Kiem District, not far from the Old Quarter. This restaurant serves excellent American food, cold craft beer, and offers a wide selection of cocktails and imported spirits that are uncommon in this part of the world. Once serving almost exclusively expats and diplomats, the Smokehouse has become popular among the Vietnamese community, too; now, they receive a good mix of locals and foreigners. Teddy's American Grill House is another popular restaurant that expats frequent. Chops, which serves up tasty burgers, beer, and great macaroni and cheese with a local twist, has branches in Tay Ho, Hoan Kiem, and Ba Dinh districts; all of them are usually full of regular customers, both foreign and Vietnamese.

One of the nicest things about Hanoi is the many lakes and parks in the city. The most famous of these is Hoan Kiem Lake ("Lake of the Returned Sword") in the city center. This tree-lined lake contains the iconic "Turtle Tower" island and the photogenic Ngoc Son Temple ("Temple of the Jade Dragon") on the northern end. The lake is encircled by walking paths and park benches. Across the street are coffee shops, popular with anyone coming to an area who wants to rest their feet and gaze upon the peaceful scene. Hoan Kiem Lake has been called the "Heart of Hanoi," and it is a must-see place for anyone coming to the city. For residents, it is a place to relax, chat with other expats, and help Vietnamese students practice their English.

Vietnam has a distinctive coffee culture, and Hanoi has hundreds, if not thousands, of coffee shops. Many of these places also serve smoothies, fresh-squeezed juices, and light snacks. Not only are these wonderful places to sit and watch the world go by, they are also perfect venues for meeting other people. You will have the best luck finding other foreigners to chat with at the coffee shops around Hoan Kiem Lake. Cong Ca Phe and Highlands Coffee, in various locations throughout the city, are two homegrown chains that attract a mixed local and foreign clientele. The ancient village of Duong Lam, the birthplace of two of Vietnam's great historic kings, is less than two hour's drive west of Hanoi, but it is a world away from the bustling city.

The village is about 1,200 years old and the oldest houses still in use date back to 1649. There are more than 950 ancient houses and 21 relic sites in and around the town, most of them made from bricks of burnt-ochre clay taken from local ponds. There is an imposing gothic Catholic Church here that was built by the French during their colonial rule of Vietnam, and Phung Hung Temple, Ngo Quyen Temple, and the multi-tiered Mia Pagoda are just five minutes from the village center. These are active places of worship; you will smell the incense and see devotees praying at the altars. Ba Vi National Park is just eight miles from Duong Lam. A steep and winding road makes its way toward Ba Vi Mountain's 4,252-foot-high summit. The tropical vegetation gradually gives way to pine forests and noticeably cooler temperatures. Along the way, you will pass by a small restaurant that offers jaw-dropping views of the Red River Valley far below.

The road continues its ascent past the ruins of a Catholic church to a parking area, where two trails lead to the top of the mountain. The steep trail on the left leads to a temple honoring Ho Chi Minh, while the shorter trail on the right ascends to a second summit with an 11th-century shrine dedicated to the Mountain God. On a clear day, the view is superb; on a foggy day, it is eerie.

The UNESCO World Heritage Site of Trang An is less than two hours from Hanoi. Take a trip on a rowboat, expertly maneuvered by local women, past dramatic limestone cliffs, solitary Buddhist temples and pagodas, lush jungle foliage, isolated fields, and deep valleys. Be sure to watch for mountain goats perched precariously on the cliffs. Depending on the season, the river flows through up to nine caves. These are not caves that you explore on your own; you'll be in the rowboat the entire time. Some of the caves are quite long, and it takes several minutes to reach the other side. Nearby Tam Coc is also part of the UNESCO complex. It offers a similar river and cave experience, but tends to receive more tourists than Trang An. You could easily visit both rivers in a day. Cuc Phuong National Park is Vietnam's oldest national park but typically receives few visitors—surprising considering all the park has to offer. Immerse yourself in the largest remaining virgin rainforest in Vietnam among 350-foot-tall trees, wild orchids, and thousands of butterflies. Trek to hidden waterfalls, climb to the 2,133-foot summit of Silver Cloudy Peak, relax on the shore of a scenic lake surrounded by nature, or explore caves containing sea fossils and the remnants of prehistoric man.

Cuc Phuong also hosts rescue and rehabilitation centers for endangered pangolins, jungle cats, primates, and turtles. Access is restricted to these centers, but a guide can be arranged at the visitor center. Volunteer opportunities are often available. You could visit Cuc Phuong as a long day trip, though it is better to stay overnight. The lodge next to the visitor center has simple, comfortable rooms, where you can relax in the evening and wake up to the otherworldly songs of the park's gibbons. The little-known Thanh Chuong Viet Palace is near the town of Soc Son, less than an hour from Hanoi. The extensive collection of art here represents the life's work of the celebrated painter Thanh Chuong, but the best parts of the palace are the grounds. When wandering the paths, you will pass small lotus-filled ponds stocked with lazy, red koi fish. There are towering pagodas, Buddhist temples guarded by horses rather than the traditional dragons, twisting bonsai, and hundreds of stone, wood, bronze, and ceramic statues. A tree might have a little red Buddha nestled among its branches; stone horses, water buffalos, elephants, dragons, and whimsical statues of soldiers, workers, and farmers rest under the shade of the leafy tropical foliage.

Around the ponds and elsewhere on the grounds, you will find intricately carved Buddha statues standing guard over pots filled with burning incense. Traditional wooden houses offer quiet areas to sit and relax or have a cup of tea. The surrounding area is green and mountainous, full of bamboo, lush tropical plants, and trees. The former French hill station of Tam Dao, just 50 miles northwest of the city, perches at a lofty 3,051 feet and is noticeably cooler than Hanoi. On a clear day, you can see across the Red River Delta, and when the fog rolls in each evening, the clouds seem to chase each other around the mountainside as if they were alive. The effect is magical! Tam Dao National Park is just a 10-minute drive from the town center. You can walk through the forest in solitude; it is not a busy park, and you likely will not run into another soul. A steep paved trail leads down from the Mela Hotel to a pretty waterfall, and there is an interesting Buddhist temple just five minutes or so from town.

Tam Dao is an excellent day trip from Hanoi, but if you want to watch the evening fog, you'll find plenty of hotels where you can spend the night.

The Perfume Pagoda is a large temple complex just a couple of hours from Hanoi. No roads lead to the site; instead, rowboats take visitors and devotees past several busy Buddhist temples to the base of the main complex. Hundreds of steps lead up to the Perfume Pagoda; it is an arduous climb. Alternately, a cable car is available to ferry passengers to the top and back. The cave that houses the main temple is massive, with high ceilings and huge formations. Many people in the north try to visit it at least once a year—usually in early spring during the Huong Pagoda Festival—to pray for health and good fortune. The cave is impressive, and the temples at the base are worth exploring, too. There is an area near the base where monks will prepare "temple food" for you—delicious vegetarian cuisine at a reasonable price. Hanoi offers mystery and intrigue around every corner. Vietnam's capital city is a fascinating mix of historical influences: traditional Chinese medicine dispensaries stocked with enigmatic herbs, grand French colonial-era mansions colored with the patina of age, traditional markets that are the same now as they were a century ago, and more motorbikes than you have probably seen in a lifetime.

Here are some of my top picks for exploring this vibrant city: The Old Quarter, in the city center, is a jumble of streets clogged with bicycle vendors, little motorbikes, cars, and food vendors, all busy on their way to somewhere. The energy here is palpable. Wander past hidden temples tucked into alleyways, exotic traditional markets, and fantastic street food. Exploring the Old Quarter is a delight for the senses; wherever you go, you will find a photograph waiting to be taken. It is the perfect place to begin your exploration of the city. Hanoi's much-loved Hoan Kiem Lake is an easy walk from the Old Quarter. Wander along the footpaths surrounding the lake, past mature shade trees, and flower gardens. At the northern end of the lake, a graceful red wooden bridge leads to Ngoc Son Temple (Temple of the Jade Mountain). You will see Thap Rua (Turtle Tower), built in 1886, on a small island at the south end of the lake. The entire area around the lake turns into a pedestrian-only zone every weekend.

This drink—a combination of strong Vietnamese coffee, sweetened condensed milk, and whipped egg yolk—tastes much better than it sounds. The milk and egg combine to form a thick and foamy marshmallow-like meringue, which is carefully floated on top of the coffee. Café Giang is the most famous venue—they've been brewing this delectable treat since 1946. This thoughtful interactive museum shows the roles that Vietnamese women have played in history, the arts, and in family life. Galleries highlight the role of women in wartime Vietnam, the incredible textiles and clothing made by ethnic minority women, and the evolution in the daily life of Vietnamese women today. It's one of the best museums in Vietnam. If you're interested in learning about the 54 ethnic minorities living in Vietnam, or contemplating making a trip to the northern or central highlands to visit some of the minority villages, the Vietnam Museum of Ethnology is well worth seeing. This carefully curated museum has many indoor and outdoor exhibits, including full-scale, traditionally built replicas of the distinctive houses and lodges of Vietnam's major ethnic minorities. Descriptive signage accompanies each exhibit. Vendors at the massive four-story Dong Xuan Market sell everything from fresh fish and produce to textiles, tools, appliances, clothes, and souvenirs. If it exists, it's probably sold here, but be prepared to bargain. Bun Cha—a delicious meal of marinated char-grilled pork, grilled ground pork patty, rice vermicelli, fresh herbs, and sweetened fish sauce—is served throughout Hanoi. Former President Obama had it and a few beers with Anthony Bourdain at the Bún Chả Hương Liên Restaurant, and so can you. There's even an altar inside honoring their visit.

The Vietnam Military History Museum has an extensive collection of exhibits. The indoor galleries focus primarily on the French and Chinese conflicts; the outdoor exhibits include quite a collection of U.S. aircraft captured or shot down during the American War. The iconic Flag Tower of Hanoi, built in 1812, is on the same grounds as the museum. Vietnamese beef noodle soup, or phở bò, is one of Hanoi's most famous dishes. Pull up a tiny chair on the sidewalk and have a steaming bowl at Phở Bò Khôi Hói in the Old Quarter. They have been serving this dish for generations; the beef marrow broth is rich and flavorful, and it is served with generous portions of beef and rice noodles. The National Fine Arts Museum has a sprawling collection of art ranging from early history through the present day. It is housed in a beautiful French colonial-era mansion that was once a Catholic girl's boarding house. The Tran Quoc Pagoda, on the causeway that separates West Lake from Truc Bach Lake, is Hanoi's oldest Buddhist temple. It has been an active place of worship since its construction in the sixth century. The 11-story pink pagoda on the grounds is lovely.

Chapter 3

Chi Biu, Bando's bookkeeper, after her arrival, their company started to grow much more money and makes them to be a great player in the Jewelry industry. Chi Biu is a 35 years old accountant from Hanoi. From the outside, she does not seem like a woman with the golden touch. But with little family and few friends, professional success is the only thing Chi devoted her time to. She is a street tough woman that is very good in accounting. Chi have made herself a good book keeper with a touch of how to make money. Bando Jewelry is not the first business Chi have turned around. Her previous work and other small companies rapidly transformed bottom line from red to black. When Bao finds out that Chi is looking for a new job, he does not waste any time making her an offer. Bao hired her as his accountant. After very short period of time, they saw that sales were growing. There was an increase in sales by forty per cent in one year. Bao and Chau make sure that Chi is very well compensated for all her hard work. Even doubling her salary over the course of a few years.

There are also exceptionally generous with gifts like first class cavations. She has a very good trips abroad, driving a nice car with all the salary that she was making. With business increasing, the couple also give their talented bookkeeper another person to be assisting her, Chien Tran, her friend, to be working with her. Chien Tran has a little bit of accounting background. She is a friend to Chi and goes to work to assist Chi. Chien helps Chi to keep the book balance and the profit flowing in. But Chien and Chi are not just co-workers and friends, they also shared a secret that can become so dangerous to both of them. They are actually lovers. Chi was a loner and she was missing the closeness of somebody in her life. Chi and Chien have something in common. Because of that, they became lovers. Chi is a loner, a middle age woman, she has very few friends, and some how Chien Tran befriends her.

Chi also becomes very obsessed with Chien, because there is nobody else in her life. She does not have any children. She never has any visitors, so Chien is very important to her. Working at Bando, allows the lovers to spend time together, and even travel as a couple. Chien and Chi have traveled to Europe together, they both work at the same place. They are best of friends. Bando Jewelry success has given everyone involved with the company a chance to enjoy the good life. But not everything as it seems to be on the surface. Chi has a secret that could ruin many lives. Secret powerful enough to drive someone to unimaginable act of violence. Chi have come a long way from her mother's upbringing in Hanoi. She is a highly skilled book keeper and a successful Hanoi Jewelry business. Her love life is full with erotic and romantic trips with her girl friend Chien Tran who works with her. But they are both keeping a dangerous secret. Chien Tran is not just Chi's lover, she is married. Chien and her husband Dung Tran, are well known in the Chinese community in Hanoi city. Edward is a true immigrant success story. He has made a fortuned in banking and he is well respected in the business world.

But image is everything. His wife's secret lesbian affair with Chi could ruin Dung Tran. But Chien and Chi forbidden adulterous affairs is the only part of lives that crosses dangerous boundaries. On the surface, Bando Jewelry with Chi help is like a very healthy business. But its success story starts to seem too good to be true. The sudden upswing of Bando's fortunes have been sp dramatic that it raise a suspicion of the authorities. The police detectives is launching investigation into the company. The deeper they look, the more they believe that Chi Biu is behind what so ever is going on at Bando Jewelry. Because she is the accountant, she is clearly one of the suspect. She could be doing this on her own without letting other people knowing. What financial investigators find when they starts to examine Bando Jewelry spreadsheet, looks like it could be a classic Ponzi scheme. The investigators discovers that Bando Jewelry is not actually making any profit. They are simply taking bank loans, written against fake orders for jewelries. Bando then uses each of this loans as a collateral to get the next loan from another bank. Therefore, you borrow money against the invoices and you are telling the person you borrowed money from that you have all these real legit customers who is going to give you back this money. You pay old bills with new money. And to pull more off you have to expand the scheme. It is a pyramid, as it keeps going, and keeps going and you can always pay back by the next loan. The person creating this elaborate paper is the bookkeeper with the magic touch, Chi Biu.

She is the one applying for the loans, and presenting banks with records of fraud incomes. When the investigators look more closely into her past, they found out that Chi has used some very creative accounting strategies, at several of her former jobs. Maybe from the various employment she had. She tried to cook the books a little and then the money started coming in. She is somehow, almost like an addiction. She was hooked up and started to like the money, the easy money. Bao and Chau believes that if they really want to get more money, they need somebody who is a little bit corrupted to cook the book, then they get Chi. At Bando, it becomes apparent that the Ponzi scheme is joggling millions of dollars to fake assets. Given the scope of the fraud, it seems unlikely, that Chi is managing it alone. Right next to her all day long is her girlfriend and companion, Chien Tran. You have to have somebody you can trust if you are creating this kind of scheme, and Chien could be trusted by Chi. The investigators reaches out to questioned Chi, but she is not willing to talk. She knows she has covered her tracks, and she does not think there is any solid evidence that investigators can act on.

She believes she is just too smart. But as the investigators presses harder on Chi to tell all of Bando's Jewelry financial secret, a truly shocking event hits Chi at full force. Her girlfriend Chien Tran suddenly goes missing. Chien's car is found abandoned, and the last place eye witness can trace her is at Chi's apartment. In March, Chien Tran has disappeared. No one heard a word from her. She was just gone, vanished. Chi Tran is worried and has become desperate to find her missing friend and lover. She is working very hard to locate her and find out what has happened to her. Chi has been posting missing person flyers about Chien Tran all over the city. There is a secret in Chien's life that could have put her at risk, and it is the same secret that Chi has. Involvement in the questionable accounting scheme at Bando Jewelry is now under thorough investigations, and her forbidden lesbian affair that could have ruined her husband,

Dung Tran. Chi Biu's world is turning from a very success story into a cloud of secret threats. However, no one could have imagine how dangerous and violent her life was about to become.

It's May 20, 1984, and Chien Tran, book keeping assistant at Bando's Jewelry has been missing since January. In the the five months Chien has gone missing, Chi has become more and more terrified that the secret they shared are the reason for Chien's disappearance. Now, a man taking an early morning walk on the downtown city street makes a terrible discovery. He found a dead woman covered with cloths, and immediately calls the police. When the police arrives, they do a quick examination of the scene. It appears as if the woman has been shot at the back of the head, and then dumped in front of an old storefront. The victim has no identification on her. Could this be the missing Chien? But when the police checked at their station, they soon discovered that she fits the description of the woman who has been abducted from a Hanoi city parking lodge Just the day before. It was a shocking bracing attack from the middle of a busy area. When three strangers tried to stop the abduction, two were shot and killed. The lone surviving witness tells police that the kidnapped woman was driven away in a van. According to eye witness, the police was looking for a woman who dressed the way the dead woman was dressing. She matched the age and basic description. One chilling details helps police to match up the two crimes. The woman being abducted lost both of her shoes when she was pulled into the van. The victim lying dead at the store front is missing both shoes. The police wore the dead woman the shoes and they fits in like Cinderella. The police said, we got it. The woman was the 35 years old Chi Biu, Bando Jewelry accountant.

The police investigating the murder are at first completely stunned that a woman like Chi has been attacked with this kind of extreme violence. This type of victim is very unusual. She has been living an interesting risky life style. The police wondered why would that happened. The detectives searched Chi's apartment, in the hope of collecting any possible evidence. There they find pictures of her lover with the still missing Chien Tran. Neighbours confirmed their two relationships and the detectives soon discover that Chien had been married while she was Chi Biu's lover. This immediately created a possible motive on the part of Dung Tran because he recently finds out that his wife is not only having an affair with a woman, but that Chien has been missing for months is even more troubling. The investigators decided to bring in Dung Tran for questioning. He did not seem particular concern that Chi has been murdered. He did not seem concern that his wife was missing. That raise questions that what he knew that he was not telling. Dung Tran behavior suddenly raised a red flag for the detectives. He claims that he did not know that Chien and Chi were having an affair. Although he has not seen Chien in months, he does not seem to care about her where about.

To the police, it was a very strange reaction. But one might be explained by cultural differences. The detectives felt that if Dung Tran has known about her wife's lesbian affairs, he would have done everything to keep it secret. He has a tremendous amount of losing his community if the truth came out. The Chinese community would not have trusted him anymore and he would have been completely embarrassed. He would probably need to relocate to somewhere else and start all over again. He could probably lose his job. Although he has a strong motive, police finds no evidence that Dung Tran was involved in any crime. Witnesses cannot place him at the scene of Chi's adoption, and there are no sign of violence in Chien Tran's disappearance. There was no evidence that the investigations could link Dung Tran to Chi Biu's murder. Since they have no other suspect, the detectives went back to the crime scene at the parking lodge, hoping to unravel how Chi kidnapping was accomplished. Soon they come across something suggestive. Records indicated that access to the parking lodge was restricted. It was a monthly parking only and no room was given to hourly parking. They found out that Chi Biu has bought a parking space for her Car. About the same time, a van had bought a parking space. The van was in and out approximately the same time Chi was in and out. This van is the same type of vehicle which last seen in the garage with Chi Biu trapped inside. The detectives determined a man named Dhin Kim, rented the parking space. Kim is a building contractor with low-level connections to organized crime. He has been a suspect in several robberies in the past. Kim's movement in and out of the parking lodge proved to be the suspect. It shows that he was watching Chi and studying what she does everyday. But his connection to the garage is still circumstantial. The detectives need more concrete evidence to tie Kim to the crime. They soon come up with a clever but unorthodox plan. The police did not have enough evidence to neither arrest him nor search his van. But they also did not want him to slip through their fingers. Because Kim has once listed his van as stolen, but he never told the police that he has gotten it back. The police now sees the vehicle as stolen property, and conducts a thorough search. Inside the van, they found 22 caliber shell case. The same type of bullet used in killing Chi Biu. Ballistic test also reveals that Kim gun was also used in the murder. The police now believed that Dhin Kim was the shooter. But why they pondered. Kim and Chi do not seem to have met, and they have no clear connection to one another. The police theorized that someone must have contracted Kim to kill Chi. But who could have wanted her dead so badly.

Kim is arrested for Chi's murder. But after hours of questioning, he still would not say a word about the crime to the police. The investigators returns to the possibility that Dung Tran, the wealthy husband to Chi's lover Chien Tran, could be behind the execution. Dung Tran had the means to do anything he wants to do, if he had the money. But from all set and done, the police still discovered that Dung Tran has nothing to do with Chi's murder. Even though they have the trigger man, police still do not know who is behind Chi's execution. But the investigations is still push to an entirely new direction. The financial investigators called on the police that Chi is still under investigations for financial crimes.

In fact, the financial investigators said that the secret she knew about the Ponzi scheme in Bando Jewelry, were a very good reason why Chi may have been killed. So the police realized that Chi was under financial investigation. The financial investigators also realized that one of their key people in the embezzlement case was now dead. After looking deeper into the Bando's book, the investigators have come to suspect that the Ponzi scheme has been going on for some time, before Chi Biu arrives. Although, Chi certainly played a key role in expanding the fraud in Bando Jewelry. It seems very likely to investigators that the person originally behind this scam is Bao Pham,

Bando's owner. He drives fancy cars, he owns fancy and expensive house, he went on lavish vacations and all these things cost money.

Chapter 4

The kind of money that he was legitimately making from Bando Jewelry would not have supported those kind of lavish life style. So he thought a creative book keeping is the best way to go. But white collar crime is one thing. It is hard for the investigators to imagine that Bao could be involved in anything like the extreme violence of Chi Biu execution. There is no criminal history about Bao Pham. He has an upstanding life and part of the community. He runs a business, he is married with two children. He is now walking in the violent side of the criminal law. Chi Biu knew too many secrets about an elaborate financial scam. But who could have been willing to undertake murder for hire to keep her from talking. After Chi Biu was kidnapped, then murdered by Dhin Kim, a man she never met, the investigators revealed something staggering. Chi was under investigation in a more time million dollar Ponzi scheme being run by Bando Jewelry.

But given the amount of money at stake, the investigators believe that the Bando Jewelry's owner, Bao Pham, was socially ambitious. He wanted flashy cars, he wanted beautiful, expensive and fancy houses. He wanted nice things. The investigators began to put the pieces together. Bao has been running the scheme for some time before he hired Chi Biu to keep the company's book. That is when he went looking for an accountant, who could run several sets of books, and could funny things up. That is when he discovered Chi Biu. So he hired her. She quickly knew exactly what he wanted, and she was very good at it. Chi's ability to make the book looked correct offered Bando the legitimately it needs. The financial investigators believe that the book keeper and the Bando leader reach an understanding that will bring them both a fortune in stolen profits. This is a huge secret that Chi would wanted to keep under her laps, for her own freedom and liberty, not to mention her reputation. But nothing stays secret forever. Eventually, the scale of the fraud going on in Bando Jewelry came to the attention of the authorities. When you get greedy, mistakes happens.

The banks finally realized that something is fishing for Bao and Chau. Eight five months before Chi's death, the auditors first arrived but Chi refuses to answer any of their questions. But Bao knows precisely what to tell the auditors. Bao was pinning the whole scheme on Chi. He says he hired her to do the book keeping job and what she is doing he does not know. He took the steps to show that Chi is embezzling from the company and she is the one responsible for any Ponzi scheme, and he knows nothing. Once Chi Biu realized that she has been set up to be the eye in the storm, she understands that her only chance to escape jail is to cooperate with the investigators and provides them with evidence that Bao is running a Ponzi scheme. So she does just that. Chi was telling the investigators on phone that she would give them all the information that they need. She would show them the books, the paper trail and tell them where all the money is.

She was not also stupid. She was keeping a set of books for herself incase anything happens to her, the police can know the truth. She has realized early, that Bao was going to use her as the fore guy. She was determine not to be the fore guy. But before she can provide hard evidence to the investigators, Chi Biu would come crashing down. Her girl friend Chien Tran turns up missing. She fears, she will be next. By the time she went to the investigators, she did not believe that her life was in danger. It was not until Chien Tran disappeared that her fears were raised. Chi never had time to give the investigators the evidence the needed to prosecute Bao for the Ponzi scheme. She ended dead before she can talk. The investigators are almost certain that Bao is behind Chi's murder. But they have no way to tie him to the killing. Although, Chi was cooperating with the police to provide evidence against Bao, but the police have no evidence yet to tie Bao to the murder. With Chi Biu's death, the police have no access to the real financial evidence of Bao Pham's role in the Ponzi scheme.

The only thing that the police know for certain is that Kim is the man who abducted and shot Chi Biu. He is their only solid link to the person behind the crime. The police pour everything they know about Kim again. The pyramid scheme at Bando Jewelry has finally been brought to light. The investigators feel certain that the man behind is Bao Pham who ordered a hit on Chi Biu to prevent her from talking to the police. But investigators still cannot make a connection between Bao and the trigger man Dhin Kim. Physical evidence connects Kim to the murder, but some circumstantial evidence connects Bao to the murder. Dhin Kim is quickly tried and convicted in the death of Chi Biu, and the two innocent bystanders who tried to come to her aid. He gets an additional jail term for conspiring to murder Chi's girl friend, Chien Tran, who is still never been found. But even with life in prison hanging over his head, Kim still kept his secrets, who hired him to kill Chi Biu and Chien. The police wenr back to the evidence in Kim's file. Looking for the smallest possible detail that might been over looked. Going over his phone records, they found a phone call made to his lawyer, Bach Than

It seems Bach have one primary client, Bao. Could Bach finally be the connection investigators have been looking for? The connection seems to be Bach. Two detectives started following Bach every day. He knew that he is being followed. The technic works. The investigators visited Bach for questioning. They told him that they do not think that he was involved in the murder of Chi but he knows something. That he has one choice, to cooperate with them or they will find a way to implicate him to the murder, and he might go to jail. He was offered immunity to tell what he knew. And Bach said that when it comes to murder and all these bodies, everything was orchestrated by Bao Pham. Bach also explain to the authorities that when the financial regulators first came to Chi, saying that Bao was trying to lay the Ponzi scheme sorely on her, Chi decided to fight back.

In her mind, she was seeking how to protect herself. Chi makes copies of the incriminating transactions, hides them in a secure location and she tells Bach exactly what she had done. By keeping copies of the cooked books, she could prove that there is really no money in the company. She made that straight to Bao. She told Bao that he could not deal with her because she had all the records to put him down. Chi told Bao that if he touches her, the police would come down on him. However, Chi has made a terrible miscalculation, by threatening to expose Bao. She is giving him a motive to kill her. It was a very bad decision she took by letting Bao knows that she had evidence to put him down. Bao was out of control and paranoid, believing that everybody was out there trying to get him. When Bao finally discovered that Chi has the paper trail, and working with the police, he was ready to keep things secret and kill all evidence. When you are a psychopath, you are not thinking straight. You are thinking I can go through this. I am not going to jail. I own the money that I stole.

Bao calls his lawyer, Bach Than, into his office to discuss the solutions that he thinks that will solve all his problems. So he said to Bach, do you know people that do things so that people can stop talking? Bao's plan was to kill both Chi and Chien, and say that they have disappeared with his fortunes and Jewelries if anyone should ask. With both women gone, no one will be able to prove his role in the scam. Bao is willing to kill two women he worked closely with, so his secrets stay hidden and all of Cando's money stays in his pocket. Bach also managed some properties in the city and one of his tenant is Dhin Kim, the man who murdered Chi Biu. Bach discovers that Kim needs money and he is willing to do things for money. So he introduced Kim to Bao. After Bao and Kim met, Chien Tran went missing, and Chi Biu is kidnapped and murdered. Any one that can connect Bao to the Ponzi scheme, is silenced forever.

To avoid being linked to the crime, Bach repeats his stories to the Jury in the law court. In return, the lawyer who connected the killer to Bao, walks free because of his cooperation with the police. Bach's story in the law court helps set Bao Pham, life in prison for the murder of Chi Biu and Chien Tran. When Chi's family finds the sets of falsified books she hid away, Bao was also convicted of financial fraud and tax evasion. His wife Chau, is sentenced to four years for her role in the Ponzi scheme. Chi Biu the Bando's book keeper came a long way from her humble beginning, but paid the ultimate price for her boundless ambition. Chien Tran body is never found and her husband Dung Tran, was never charged with any crime.

About the Author

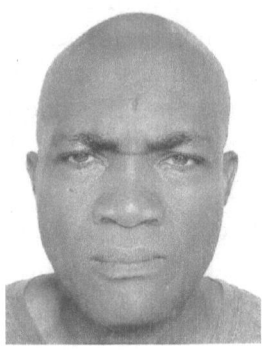

Bright Mills

Bestselling author Bright Mills is a writer, an engineer and a historian from Nigeria. He has a degree in Information Technology. He is a creative writer and have written so many books in Fiction and nonfiction. His books have received starred reviews weekly, library journal, and Book list. He promises to pull heartstrings, offer a few laughs, and share tidbits of tantalizing history. Many have praised his work.

www.ingramcontent.com/pod-product-compliance
Lightning Source LLC
LaVergne TN
LVHW041552070526
838199LV00046B/1923